Advanced Dungeons&Due

Official Game Adventure

An Adventure for 4-5 Characters, Levels 3-6

The Elephanzion

Written by Daniel Anderson of the Bugbear Brothers

Credits

Writing: Daniel Anderson, with
    contributions from
    Cameron Foster

Cover Art: Britt Martin

Interior Art: Cameron Foster,
    Carlos Castillo

Graphic Design: Eric Smith

We claim no ownership or rights, whatsoever, to Advanced Dungeons & Dragons, the AD&D logo, TSR, Inc., the TSR, Inc. logo, or the phrase Products of Your Imagination.

Table of Contents

TSP, Inc.
PRODUCTS OF YOUR FASCINATION™

Introduction

The Elephanzion is a beginning adventure for 4–5 characters of 3rd to 6th level. The adventure is set in a nondescript jungle environs that can be easily transplanted into any fantasy setting. The adventure was designed for Dungeons & Dragons Fifth Edition, but can easily be modified for any fantasy tabletop roleplaying game system.

Stat Blocks

In order to play this adventure, you will need access to the Dungeons & Dragons Fifth Edition *Monster Manual*. Monsters and NPC's with stat blocks that can be found in the manual will be **bolded** throughout the adventure. Homebrewed monsters' stat blocks will be included where they appear in the adventure.

Setup

Two weeks prior to the planned start date of the *Elephanzion* campaign, discreetly obtain the physical mailing addresses of all the attending players. You may want to get into contact with mutual friends or their partners if you want them to be surprised. Next, send each player an invitation to the Bloodbath Jubilee without including any return address information on the envelope. If questioned about the letter, strongly deny any involvement.

Invitation

See page 5.

Optional Reasons to Enter the Elephanzion

Gordon Saint's Disappearance. Gordon Saint, a notorious carnie who travels between towns with his collection of bizarre and otherworldly wonders, has gone missing while visiting the region. One of his telltale belongings, a signature black top hat, was found discarded near the entrance to the Elephanzion.

The Hunt for the Moonplate Set. Legends tell of an enchanted set of magical items which once belonged to a moon warrior of great renown, Ozymandias. Rumours suggest that the three artifacts he once owned might be found within the jungle temple, waiting to be discovered.

Rescue Raithvus Spane. An orog war wizard, who has been conscripted by the Bronze Legion, has gone missing while travelling to the eastern front. The reward for rescuing him alive is a share of all future contracts the powerful spellcaster signs.

Stopping the Troll Infestation. Trolls are multiplying in the area. Many have been spilling out of the jungles surrounding the Elephanzion.The presence of a troll den or burrow is likely the culprit. Locate the source of the infestation and bring back six fresh troll ears to prove it.

Confronting Evil in Desecrated Lands. The growing presence of fiends on the material plane has angered the gods, causing all Paladin and Cleric divine magic to have a 25% of failing within a 100-mile radius of the temple. Go root out the source of this evil and destroy it. If you choose this reason as the basis for your campaign, have all divine spellcasters roll 1d4 whenever they wish to cast a spell, on a result of '1' their spell fails. This condition will persist until Ovallo is killed.

THE ELEPHANZION

1. The Front Entrance

The Elephanzion is a massive sandstone temple sequestered deep within steep labyrinthine foothills. The surrounding region is dense with an assortment of kapok trees, verdant ferns and towering palms. The temple is a historic tribute to the Elephant God, Phantrenei, and is an impressive structure that exudes symmetry from every angle.

At the centre of the structure lies a large, broken fountain. The fountain is flanked by four access points to the temple. Two curved staircases lead up to the sides of the temple, granting access to the arena seating within. In addition, two sloped ramps provide a straight path up to the stone platform lying before the temple's front gate. A DC 15 Strength (athletics) check is necessary to wrench open the temple's aged wooden doors.

1.B Temple Interior: The Viewing Gallery

As one passes through the gate, they will come across a suspended viewing gallery that hangs over a long sporting arena. The gallery is furnished with three offset thrones, which are situated on a precipice overlooking the arena. Narrowing, tusk-shaped stairs flank each side of the gallery, leading down towards the court. When looking back at the entrance from the arena below, one can see a trunk carved flush beneath the

Dear   ,

I hope this correspondence finds you well. I write to extend you an invitation to this year's Bloodbath Jubilee. You are cordially invited to witness a showcasing of debauchery, revelry, sin and sacrifice unlike no other—may your carnal appetites be fully satiated. I sincerely hope you will be able to attend and enjoy a scrumptious repast. I have no doubt you will enjoy the company of other attendees, the stimulating conversations that will undoubtedly unfold, and the delightful victuals provided.

Due to unforeseen circumstances, the event's traditional location has changed. Please arrive at the following location and time:

Address:
Date:
Time:

Sincerely,

Ovallo

gallery, and massive ears carved into the walls on either side, depicting the head of an elephant.

Beneath the foremost throne's seat, there is a set of three magic runes, which can be located with a DC 18 Intelligence (investigation) check. If one runs their hand over the runes, an arcane shield envelops the entire arena, instantly containing the events within, and simultaneously causes six portcullises against the east and west walls to lift. Running one's hand over the runes a second time releases this powerful ward and lowers the portcullises.

1.C Temple Interior: The Arena
The exterior of the temple features two staircases which lead towards parallel entrances into the structure's arena seating. The oval-shaped stadium spans 70 ft. from end to end and is supported by four gargantuan pillars carved to resemble jaguars standing on their hind legs. These pillars are located just beyond the edges of the arena floor, amidst the numerous tiered benches. There is a 15 ft. drop between the front row of seating and the sandy expanse of the arena's play surface. Seven adamantine portcullises are evenly spaced around the arena, with three on each side and one at the opposite end of the front gates. While there appear to be no levers connected to the six portcullises along the east and west walls, there is a lever located next to the portcullis at the far end of the stadium. This portcullis guards a path leading toward the rear of the temple.

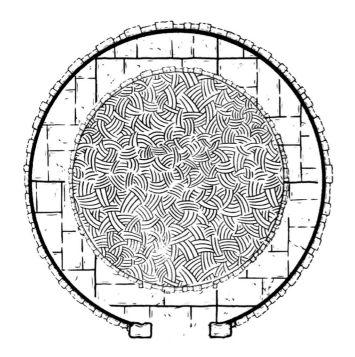

1.D Temple Interior: The Pit
Beyond the portcullis lies a circular room with a 20 ft. diameter pit at its centre and a 5 ft. wide walkway encircling it. The room's domed ceiling is severely damaged, riddled with openings and cracks that allow sunlight to stream through, which casts intricate patterns against the interior walls. The pit itself is overgrown with invasive jungle trees and bulbous vines and creepers that protrude from its sides. It descends 40 ft. and is home to a colony of five aggressive mammoth squirrels, hopping around territorially. The squirrels possess venom-tipped tusks and will attack intruders if provoked. At the pit's bottom lies a door leading to the Elephanzion's subterranean

dungeons. It is situated on the south side just above the pit room's entrance and covered in thick bramble squirrel nests. A DC 18 Wisdom (perception) check is required to spot the door from above, although it becomes immediately visible when standing at the bottom of the pit.

Mammoth Squirrel

Description: These squirrels are massive in comparison to their alpine forest counterparts, standing approximately 7 ft. tall when positioned upright on their hind legs. However, they are not intelligent and will often mistake creatures for their own kin if they are sufficiently hairy, or draped in a fur cloak.

Medium beast, unaligned

Armour Class: 13
Hit Points: 9 (3d6)
Speed: 35 ft., 30 ft. jump
Skills: Stealth +5
Senses: passive Perception 9
Challenge: 1/8 (25 XP)

Strength: +3
Dexterity: +3
Constitution: 0
Intelligence: -4
Wisdom: -1
Charisma: -3

Pounce. If the squirrel jumps at least 20 ft. onto a creature, the target must succeed on a DC 14 Strength saving throw or be knocked prone. If the squirrel successfully knocks a target prone, it may use its bonus action to perform a Tusk Gore attack.

Skull-Crushing Bite. Melee Weapon Attack: +5 to hit, reach 5 ft., one target. Hit: 6 (1d6 + 3) piercing damage. If the squirrel's bite is successful, any tiny, small or medium target must succeed on a DC 15 Constitution saving throw or drop to 0 hit points, fall unconscious, and begin making death saves with disadvantage on their next turn. A creature that becomes unconscious in this way cannot be stabilised by traditional means. If a DC 15 Wisdom (medicine) check is performed, or if the creature receives over 5 points of magical healing, they become stabilised. Any additional healing thereafter will cause the creature to regain consciousness.

Tusk Gore. Melee Weapon Attack: +5 to hit, reach 5 ft., one target. Hit: 6 (1d6 + 3) piercing damage. The target must succeed on a DC 13 Constitution saving throw or take an additional 10 (2d10) poison damage.

2. Front Lawn & Buried Siege Tower
In front of the temple lies a vast, perfectly level grass field. There is an 85 x 85 ft. square marked out by a shallow henge in the field's centre. Though not obvious to the eye, the top of a buried siege tower lies directly in the middle of the marked-off square. The tower features four levels, each measuring 10 ft. high.

Locating the tower within the henge requires a DC 15 Intelligence (investigation) check due to the ground above it being covered in mulch, entangled vines, and dead leaves. Once discovered, a 5 x 5 ft. hatch can be lifted to reveal the tower's first level. Ladders connect each level, but there is also a ceiling-anchored climbing rope found between the third and fourth levels. Putting any pressure on the first rung of the ladder between the third and fourth levels will cause a crackling moon ray to plummet from the skies and summon a Sulphur Lamia within the henge above. The rung's connection to an alarm can be identified with a DC 18 Intelligence (investigation) check. The Lamia will only appear if the henge is undamaged and will hunt down anyone wandering near or within the tower. The tower's base has a stone door leading to the Elephanzion, which is protected by warding runes carved above the door frame. While the Sulphur Lamia is prevented from pursuing beyond this point, it will continue to guard the exit until killed or until the next full moon.

Sulfur Lamia

Description: This serpentine temptress is yellow-skinned and reeks of sulphur and rot. Her eyes glow with tangerine fire and her scream is bone-chilling.

Medium fiend, neutral evil

Armour Class: 14
Hit Points: 75 (10d8 + 20)
Speed: 40 ft.
Skills: Deception +4, Perception +3, Stealth +4
Damage Resistances: acid, fire, poison
Senses: darkvision 60 ft., passive Perception 13
Languages: Common, Abyssal, Infernal
Challenge: 4 (1,100 XP)

Strength: +4
Dexterity: +2
Constitution: +2
Intelligence: +3
Wisdom: +1
Charisma: +1

Sulfuric Immolation (Recharge 5–6). Ranged Spell Attack: +5 to hit, range 60 ft., two targets. Hit: 9 (2d12 + 3) acid damage. The target(s) must succeed on a DC 13 Constitution saving throw or succumb to moon rot. Every night that the affected creature is exposed to moonlight they will begin to sublimate, as their flesh slowly drifts skyward, causing them to lose 1d4 from their maximum hit points. This will continue until the disease is cured.

Claw. Melee Weapon Attack: +6 to hit, reach 5 ft., one target. Hit: 8 (1d8 + 4) slashing damage.

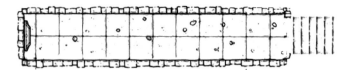

3. The Technicolour Path

Between the two ascending ramps that lead towards the temple's raised front gate is a wide staircase. This marble staircase descends 20 ft. towards a 60 ft. long walkway littered with technicolour, glimmering stones. These stones are engraved with hieroglyphics of different beasts in no discernible order (roll 1d12 per space to determine what animal is engraved on a particular stone): 1) cassowary, 2) pelican 3) hippopotamus, 4) hyena, 5) anaconda, 6) chameleon, 7) toad, 8) salamander, 9) piranha, 10) arapaima, 11) moth, and 12) cicada. A DC 15 Intelligence (nature) check can be used to identify the details and names of each of these beasts, otherwise describe the creature's features without mentioning its official title. If a creature steps on two of the same animal category in a row (bird, mammal, reptile, amphibian, fish, insect), they take 2d6 force damage from an arcane explosion. The portal at the end of the path teleports any who enter into Death Lake (4).

4. Death Lake

A giant subterranean swamp festers within an enclosed cave that spans 400 ft. from floor to ceiling. This cave system is illuminated by a small, humming grey sun that hangs exactly halfway between the ceiling and waterline. The swamp is chock full of albino hippopotamuses with lurid, red eyes. Rotting lilies and bloated fish corpses fill the air with a putrid odour, so all who enter must perform a DC 15 Constitution saving throw not to retch and vomit at the smell. Those who enter the portal at the end of the Technicolour Path (3) appear on a tiny 10 ft. diameter island. From the centre of the island to the cave wall at any point is a radius of 80 ft. A single door exists

100 ft. up on the cave wall to the east. If a creature somehow reaches the door, it teleports them into the Gleam Gate Hold (6). Otherwise, the creature's fate is likely to be the next meal of the temperamental, gaunt hippos.

Albino Hippopotamus

Description: Massive lumbering quadrupedal beasts with cleavers for teeth, white flesh and opaque, crimson eyes.

Large beast, unaligned

Armour Class: 13
Hit Points: 80 (10d10 + 30)
Speed: 35 ft.
Skills: Perception +3
Senses: blindsight; passive Perception 13
Languages: --
Challenge: 3 (700 XP)

Strength: +4
Dexterity: 0
Constitution: +4
Intelligence: -1
Wisdom: +1
Charisma: -1

Bite. *Melee Weapon Attack:* +6 to hit, reach 5 ft., one target. Hit: 24 (4d10 + 4) piercing damage and 9 (1d10 + 4) bludgeoning damage.

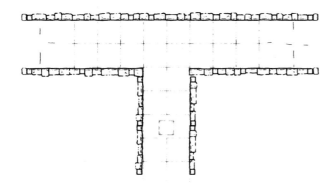

5. The Artery of Gosalamanten
The Temple Pit (1D) and Siege Tower (2) entrances are connected by a straight, 180 ft. sandstone corridor running directly beneath the temple and lawn. The corridor is adorned with ancient hieroglyphics depicting grisly sacrificial events performed by horned sadists. Halfway down this corridor is a connected, branching hallway running 30 ft. directly west.

5.B Chute Trap
15 ft. down the connected hallway is a pressure-plated chute trap that triggers if a weight greater than 50 lbs. is placed on it. The chute may be noticed with a DC 18 Intelligence (investigation) check. Once triggered, the 5 ft. triggering panel and 10 ft. of flooring preceding it will tilt down 45 degrees and lubricating oil will grease the stone, creating a slippery chute. This chute leads into a 50 ft. greased slide and drop. After the trap is triggered, the flooring will return level after a 6 second delay. Creatures standing on the floor when the trap activates must make a DC 20 Dexterity saving throw; otherwise, they will tumble down the slide and reach a 60ft. deadfall between the chute's end and the Gleam Gate Hold's (6) floor.

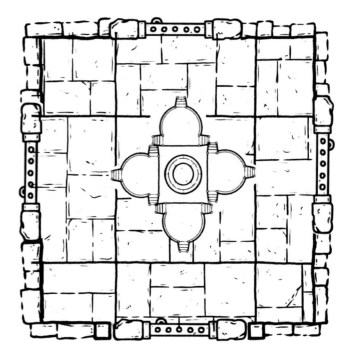

6. Gleam Gate Hold
The 60 x 60 ft. square room beneath the chute has four adamantine portcullis exits, spaced evenly along the room's four walls. Inside the room, there are four **orog** geriatrics that will attack the characters and try to kill them.

The room also has four symmetrical pedestals surrounding a statue in its center. Each pedestal contains a small, ornamental chariot statue. Each of the statues is made of a different material: bronze (though patinated and appearing to be aquamarine), black onyx, ironwood, and oxblood red china. The statue at the centre is a four-armed nephilim. The statue sits on a raised stone platform. Its intricately-patterned chest is illuminated from an angled skylight on the ceiling during the daytime hours and by moonlight at night. The statue is made of cinnabar and is vivid red: its two upper hands bear scimitars while the lower two are cupped together with their palms overlapping and facing up. If an object is placed in the statue's open hands, the statue will raise it to the centre of its chest, catching any light streaming from the skylight and directing it towards a crescent lunar symbol resting 30 ft. up on the west wall. If light does not reflect off the chosen object, the hands will lower the chariot after 12 seconds and return to their original position. The only way to get enough light into the lunar symbol's aperture is to clean off the bronze chariot, or another suitably reflective item, and hand it to the statue. When light enters the moon symbol, all four portcullises in the room will rise in unison. Anytime an incorrect chariot or item is placed in the statue's hand, time dilation occurs and one year will instantly pass. The orogs found in the room were tomb raiders that could not figure out how to exit the room and have aged forty years on account of their many failed attempts at the puzzle. When time dilation occurs, characters' hair, noses, fingernails, and ears grow at an incredible rate, dust collects on items and the bronze becomes more patinated.

Besides the bronze portal there is only one other exit to the chamber, which is a cramped ventilation shaft located on the east wall. The shaft is 10 ft. off the ground and is just big enough to fit medium-sized creatures inside. The shaft leads towards the Mound of the Fat God (19).

The North Portcullis: Leads to a pulsing, bronze portal. Any who enter appear on the Candlemoon Plains (10).

The South Portcullis: Leads to a swirling butterscotch brown portal. The portal heals a character to full health instantly but causes their cells to repair and replicate too quickly, causing an aggressive cancer that will show signs of tumours within a day, and will kill them within 1d4 months. The only way to end this effect is with the *Greater Restoration* spell or magic of a similar level of power. The portal disappears after it is used.

The East Portcullis: Leads to a flickering red portal. One who enters will exit with razor sharp tusks. The tusks deal +1 piercing damage to enemy melee combatants when you successfully hit them with another melee attack. The portal disappears after it is used.

The West Portcullis: Leads to a humming black portal. Entering transforms one's nose into a 5 ft. long trunk. The trunk may be used to grip objects up to 5 ft. away. The portal disappears after it is used.

7. The Cicada Chute

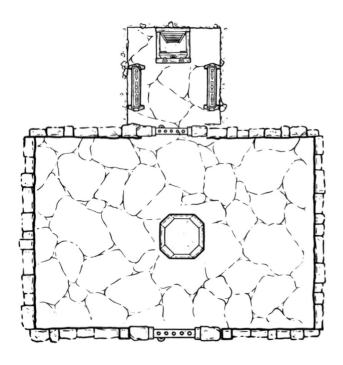

If the connected hallway's Chute Trap (5B) is somehow avoided, the corridor continues onward another 15 ft. and opens into a 40 x 40 ft. square room that contains a freestanding carapace in its centre and a door at its far end. The carapace stands 6 ft. 2 in. high and appears to be made out of a hard insectoid exoskeleton. If anyone steps inside the bizarre carapace, a set of translucent, chitinous dragonfly wings will enclose them inside and the floor beneath the carapace will drop out like a waterslide, suddenly flushing them 20 ft. down into the Cardiac Chambers (8).

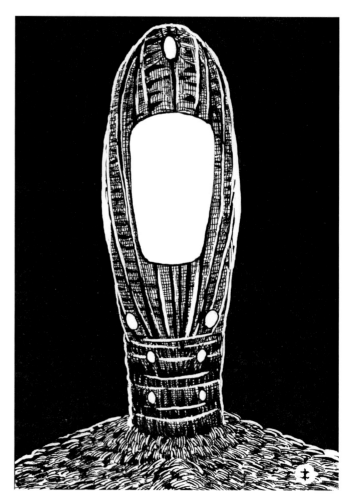

At the far end of the room is a wooden door. The door opens upon a small armoury closet with straw covering the floor. The plentiful weapons inside include three macuahuitls, two atlatls, six tomahawks, three blowguns, and four bolas. If the heather on the bottom of the closet is swept away and a DC 15 Intelligence (investigation) is performed, creatures will notice a well-concealed hatch. Beneath the hatch is a long ladder that descends directly towards the Sadist's Sanctum (12). The hidden door at the bottom of the ladder opens behind the left leg of the towering Elephant Statue found in the Sadist's Sanctum (12).

8. Cardiac Chambers

This pair of connected rooms are made out of glowing layers of thick rubbery flesh and are filled to the brim with coursing blood. Creatures must hold their breath while inside. Note that while creatures are active, they may hold their breath for a number of seconds equal to 30 plus their Constitution score (~5–8 rounds). While inactive, they may double this time. When a creature's breath runs out, they immediately

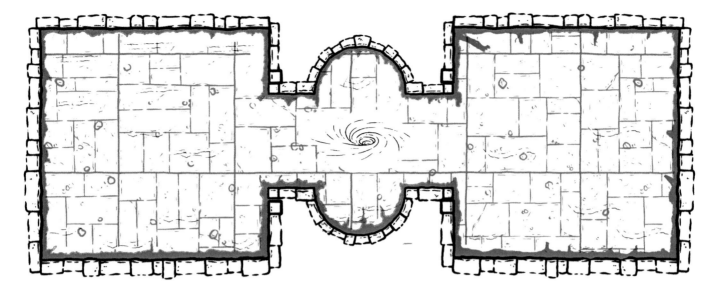

drop to 0 hit points. Every round, the two rooms contract, flushing the blood back-and-forth between the two chambers. Creatures may perform a DC 17 Strength saving throw to avoid being sucked into the other aorta. Five bloodgila eels swarm between the chambers, unaffected by these cardiac currents. The eels will attack any intruders. Between pumps, characters may notice a gilded crystalline tablet swishing back and forth between the rooms with a DC 13 Wisdom (perception) check. A DC 12 Dexterity check is required to successfully grab it. If they manage to procure the tablet, it reads:

"To and fro, froth and foam, the night king's command will choose thy home."

If a creature utters the word "Tide," a fleshy exit will materialise, and all the blood will drain, leaving the eels helplessly flopping on the ground. The exit leads to the top of the ramp in the Nautilus Room (9).

Bloodgila Eels

Description: These slimy beasts boast blade-shaped fins running their entire body lengths, with long yellow filament hanging off them. Their teeth are needles and their eyes are jet black.

Small beast, unaligned

Armour Class: 13
Hit Points: 20 (4d6 + 4)
Speed: Swim 35 ft.
Skills: Stealth +6
Senses: blindsight 30 ft., passive Perception 10
Languages: --
Challenge: 1 (200 XP)

Strength: +2
Dexterity: +4
Constitution: +1
Intelligence: -2
Wisdom: 0
Charisma: -2

Bloodlust. Bloodgila eels are attracted to the scent of blood. If a creature within 30 ft. of them takes damage that causes it to bleed, the eels can use their reaction to move their swim speed towards the source of the blood and take a free Bite action.

Bite. *Melee Weapon Attack:* +4 to hit, reach 5 ft., one creature. Hit: 7 (1d10 + 2) piercing damage. The target must succeed on a DC 11 Constitution saving throw or be paralyzed until the end of their next turn.

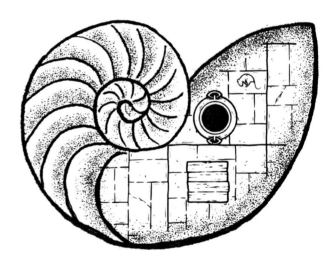

9. The Nautilus Room

The sphincter of the Cardiac Chambers (8) opens upon a wide spiral ramp that gradually narrows as it descends 180 degrees down towards a small landing. From a bird's eye view, one would realise that the room is actually the cross-section of the shell of some giant prehistoric nautilus. At the base of the ramp, there is an obese **hag** with straight purple hair, singing a haunting song as she slowly stirs a cauldron with a large wooden ladle. Beside her is a crude workbench with a dissected goblin corpse lying horizontally crucified on it and several beakers brimming with variously coloured ales. If the four compartments beneath the workbench are searched, a map can be found there. The urban map details the large troll city of "Underbridge," located beneath a giant causeway which connects two subterranean mountain ranges. On the backside of the map are the poorly scribbled lyrics to the hag's bizarre song, which she seems to keep singing compulsively. Beside the workbench is a 5 square inch indentation in the stone flooring.

The hag is territorial, disinterested in conversation, and will snarl at anyone who gets too close to her. However, she will only attack if she is harmed first. The song she perpetually sings as she splashes the horrible smelling brew with organ meat and liquids says:

"Boil, bubble
Beast of Rubble,
Bog,
Boy,
Yow,
Sing for Devils,
Squawks of Revel,
Boil, boil, bubble!"

If she is killed, or lured away from the cauldron, the characters may find a scrambled puzzle cube in the bottom of her cauldron. The cube has the following six colours: red, white, green, blue, orange and yellow. If one side's face is rearranged to read BLUE ORANGE GREEN (bog), BLUE ORANGE YELLOW (boy), YELLOW ORANGE WHITE (yow) to match the troll's song, and inserted into the cube indentation, then a steaming, freestanding crystal door, held within a bronze frame, will be lowered by chains from a hidden compartment high up in the room's ceiling.

Easy Puzzle: Tell the players that their characters see streaks of colour emanate from the cauldron during the middle section of the Hag's song. If they later remove the puzzle cube, let them see the patterns of colour light up everytime the three cypher words are spoken. To make the puzzle even easier, have the Hag's song lyrics' letters written in coloured inks corresponding to the cube and let players perform Intelligence checks to help them solve the cube itself.

Medium Puzzle: Tell the players that their characters see streaks of colour appear in the cauldron during the middle of the Hag's song but provide no further clues.

Hard Puzzle: When the characters discover the puzzle cube, produce a physical puzzle cube for the players to solve.

Instead of using the crystal door, one can also exit the room by slurping the vile brew the hag was concocting. This brew is called Troll Tequila. Once the liquid touches a creature's lips, they will appear beneath the walkway on the lower section of Mutation Row (14B), beside the door leading towards Underbridge (22).

Troll Tequila
This straw-coloured potion allows the drinker to immediately teleport to the nearest location containing a living troll. If consumed within the Elephanzion, the drinker will immediately appear in the location referenced above. There is a tequila worm floating around in the cloudy mixture. If a creature eats the tequila worm, they mutate into a pygmy troll, transforming to a height of 4 ft. tall, but acquiring all the other features of a troll, including their attribute scores, regeneration ability, and vulnerability to fire. Their maximum health will become half that of a full-grown **troll**.

9.B The Crystal Gaol
If the crystal door is opened it will reveal a small pocket dimension. This dimension appears in the form of a 65 x 65 x 40 ft. room, which contains two giant jail cells constructed

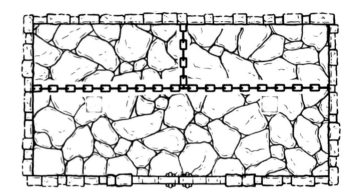

from tightly-woven adamantine wire. One jail cell contains twelve obese children, while the other is filled with half a dozen emaciated goblins.

The jails' cell doors are magically connected to square indentations in the floor in front of each respective jail cell, identical to the cube indentation that initially lowered the door from the ceiling in the Nautilus Room (9). However, the crystal door will forcefully slam closed in 6 seconds if the cube is removed from the square indentation in the Nautilus Room's (9) floor. Upon closing, the crystal door will then begin ascending back towards its ceiling compartment unless a cube is placed in it again. If the heroes wish to try to free the captives, they must figure out how to get the cube, or a suitable duplicate (via spells such as Prestidigitation), inside the room to open the jails and back out prior to the door closing. Further complicating the issue, once the cube is used to open a jail inside the Crystal Gaol, the cube will immediately disintegrate, cutting off the means of an easy exit, and leaving the prisoners of the other cell trapped.

The human children are entitled brats, interested only in when their next meal will be. The mistreated goblins, in contrast, are quite well-mannered. The goblins know about the concealed escape hatch in the pocket dimension's ceiling, sitting 40 ft. above them. This hatch opens onto the central pedestal in the Incubation Chamber (13). The goblins are illiterate, poorly spoken, and only know how to speak Goblinoid. A DC 16 Wisdom (insight) check is needed to communicate with them if no one in the party knows their tongue. If the children are searched, a perfectly white porcelain dinner plate will be found concealed in the crowd of them.

The "Table Set" Plate
Once every hour, this platter can conjure a sumptuous meal when a creature utters the phrase "table set." The troll has given this plate to the children, who prize it. They obviously have not shared any food with the goblins, who will do their best to let the characters know about its existence.

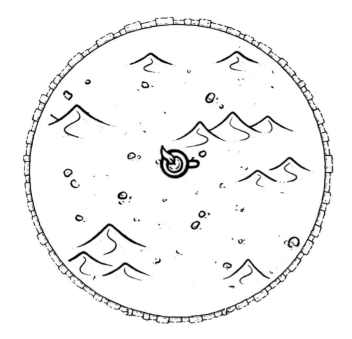

10. The Candlemoon Plains

If the heroes enter the bronze portal in the Gleam Gate Hold (6), they will emerge upon a vast gravelly plain, with sparse hills littering the barren landscape, stretched underneath a starless night sky. The only lightsource in the desolate surroundings is a gigantic free-floating candle hovering at the centre of the plains. Globs of misshapen wax drip from the candle and form an ever-growing spire of goo in the middle of the plains. The plains are 50 miles in diameter. No matter which direction one travels, they will eventually be heading back towards the centre. So long as a creature's direction of travel does not change, one will reach the plains' centre after 25 miles: that is, in approximately eight hours of travel by foot. However, unless a heat source is located, creatures take 1d4 cold damage per hour from the frigid weather.

Loitering beneath the enormous light-giving candle in the plains' centre, there is a parakeet-headed man holding up an unlit lantern. The parakeet head will remain sentient no matter what is done to the creature's body and will continue talking. Regardless of what is said to him, he will say:

"Let me tell you the story of the thousand rotting suns: Once there was a sky farmer who had two moons that did not belong. He threshed and he scythed, but the rocks would not budge. So, he collected all the lights of the evening in his basket. He hurled starfire at the pair of space stones that tormented him. The farmer was a bad shot. It took a thousand stars to finally fell the moons. And in the void beneath the rocks, those thousand stars lay there rotting–a lasting testament to his bad aim. Seeing them finally fall, the farmer smiled and sighed a breath of relief, but that's when he saw his breath draw fog. With no more suns left to throw, he froze into a statue of icy flesh, for it was not the moons that did not belong, but the farmer."

The birdman will refuse to elaborate on the meaning of his story, but if he is asked to repeat it, he will happily oblige. If the parakeet-headed man is questioned, he will prove both laconic and pithy–but will indicate the direction of the exit merely by pointing. In the direction that he points, 25 miles away, is a freestanding iron door frame. When one passes through, they appear in the Treasury (11).

11. Treasury

This 20 x 20 ft. square room is empty save for a lone chest resting in its centre and a door located at its far end, which leads to the Sadist's Sanctum (12). When opened, it will be revealed that the chest contains a pair of Cassowary Breaches. Both *Detect Good & Evil* and Identify will register the pants as possessed. Though not obvious to the eye, the pantaloons are infected by a **ghost**, called a dybbuk, which will immediately possess the first creature to touch them, without requiring the creature to perform a Charisma saving throw. The ghost will attempt to murder fellow party members while they rest but will remain dormant otherwise. The chest also contains a forest-green Panzer Potion contained in a shield-shaped, glass bottle.

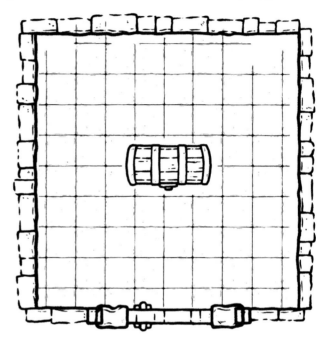

Dybbuk

Description: When untethered from body and object, this ethereal being appears as a smoky, eigengrau cord that slithers along the ground. This creature differs in two important respects from a standard **ghost**: 1) a dybbuk can automatically possess a creature that handles an object it is imbued within (no saving throw is required) and 2) a dybbuk that is exorcised from a creature, due to the host dropping to 0 hit points, may possess any unworn item it can reach with its movement as a reaction. The only way to kill a dybbuk is by incinerating the object it lives in without directly handling it and dousing the ashes of said object in holy water.

Cassowary Breaches

These chitinous insectoid pantaloons have countless cracks with chubby varicose veins poking out, surging with brilliant, violet blood. When equipped, they allow the wearer to extend their legs by up to 6 ft. as a bonus action, causing them to tower in stature and their feet to transform into cassowary talons. This condition lasts one minute. While their legs are extended in this manner, as an action, the wielder can perform a powerful kick, adding their Strength modifier and proficiency bonus to the attack roll. If the strike hits, they deal 1d4 multiplied by their current level in slashing damage. The wielder may activate the pants a number of times per long rest equal to their proficiency bonus.

Panzer Potion
This potion increases the consumer's AC by +1d10 for one minute (rolled every time the creature is hit by an attack). In addition, this potion grants the consumer +1d10 to all saving throws during that same period of time.

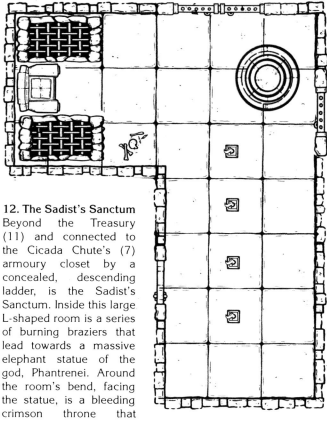

12. The Sadist's Sanctum
Beyond the Treasury (11) and connected to the Cicada Chute's (7) armoury closet by a concealed, descending ladder, is the Sadist's Sanctum. Inside this large L-shaped room is a series of burning braziers that lead towards a massive elephant statue of the god, Phantrenei. Around the room's bend, facing the statue, is a bleeding crimson throne that constantly drips and drizzles viscera into two, flanking sets of sewer grates. Sitting on the throne is the ArchDaemon of the Elephanzion: Ovallo the Unslakeable.

This **bearded devil** sports a long, braided goatee and grasps a magical bardiche. He wears an olive drab military uniform adorned in grisly medals and brightly painted yellow, blue and red chevrons. He will begin by thanking the creatures for responding to his invitation, without elaborating on what he is referring to, and then offer to tell the creatures what deadly trap lies in the dungeon, so long as they agree to stand by and watch him slit the throat of a whimpering goblin thrall cowering over in the corner of the room. The well-spoken, indignant **goblin**, who is named Patrick, will utter the following phrase:

"None can be let to draw breath if they dare besmirch the name of Lord Spane. You will pay for your insolence, miscreant!"

Every time the goblin squire speaks, the devil will draw it over to him with telekinesis (which he can cast at will) and viciously strike it, lowering its health by 1 with each hit. If the heroes refuse to witness his sacrifice, he will let them pass and will snicker as they do so, saying that "you'll be sorry." If Ovallo is attacked, he will whistle and use telekinesis to lift the metal grating beneath his throne, summoning five **barbed devils**. These devils had been drinking the spill-off from the throne. If Ovallo drops below half health, he will sprint towards the hidden chamber behind Phantrenei's left leg in an effort to ascend the ladder and escape the facility.

If the characters do agree to watch him murder the helpless goblin, he will revel in it, purposefully taking his sweet time in order to gauge the group's depravity–or lack thereof. If he surmises the party is as wicked as he is, he will provide them tickets to an event called the Bloodbath Jubilee, and request they return to the Elephanzion the next morning to witness a sacrificial celebration. Regardless of how the characters he reacts, if they agree to witness the act, he will somewhat reluctantly fulfil his end of the bargain and advise them that anyone who has touched the magical pantaloons in the previous room is cursed and to keep two watches at night until they can find a cleric (which he spits on the ground after mentioning) to cleanse them. Then he will demand they leave, seemingly sullen and pestered by a lack of stimulation.

Ovallo's Bardiche of Silent Sorrow
When this magical weapon strikes a target, they must perform a DC 15 Constitution saving throw or else suffer from the silent sorrow. Secretly hand the player a note, telling them the following:

Without revealing any information to other players, begin rolling death saves at the start of each of your subsequent turns, starting on your next turn. Though you are able to act, react and move normally during this period, if you fail three death saves before rolling three successes, then you will die instantly. Both your character and other characters are unaware of this condition and the only way to stop it is for you to receive magical healing prior to three death save failures.

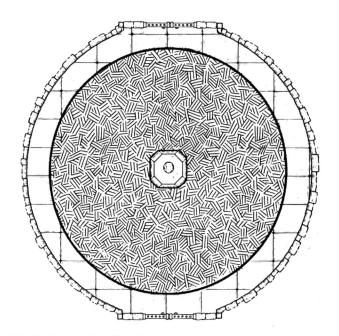

13. The Incubation Chamber
The room beyond the Sadist's Sanctum (12) is a giant railing-contained walkway that surrounds a central pedestal. The room is 300 ft. in diameter and the chasm surrounding the 10 ft. diameter pedestal is a dizzying 500 ft. deep. The pillar-supported pedestal holds an 80 lb. salmon-coloured egg. Hidden beneath the straw on the pedestal is a secret hatch to the ceiling of the Crystal Gaol (9B). Struggling and making muffled sounds on the same pedestal is a gagged and bound blue orog. This is Raithvus Spane–an infamous war **mage**.

Inside the egg is a growing Encephalon that will hatch within an hour's time from when the heroes first enter. If somehow

freed, Spane will reveal that Ovallo the Unslakeable and other decorated veteran devils, called the "Sixths of Maxoplaque," are training a menagerie of creatures to perform at an upcoming event called the Bloodbath Jubilee, set to occur the very next day. He warns that Ovallo's feigned hospitality is a ruse: they are being led deeper into the dungeon to serve as live sacrifices for the event. Raithvus knows that there is another exit to the facility at its other end. At the other end of the circular walkway is a door that leads to Mutation Row (14).

If the heroes attempt returning to the Sadist's Sanctum (12) or backtracking they will find that a patrol of five **barbed devil** slavers (if they were not killed in the Sadist's Sanctum (12)) and a shadow mastiff are prowling, looking to imprison them in the dungeon. If they are knocked unconscious or surrender, they will be imprisoned beneath Ovallo's bleeding throne and used as sacrifices in the Arena (1C) the next morning.

Raithvus Spane

Description: Spane's flesh is covered in surgical stitches and countless faint tattoos. The skin appears to be a surgical graft gone horribly wrong: it is discoloured and reeks of a putrid combination of decay and formaldehyde even from vast distances.

Raithvus Spane has the stat block of a **mage** with one exception. Because Raithvus is an orog, with robust natural stamina, he must be dealt a blow of 12 damage or higher to kill him, otherwise he remains conscious with 1 hit point.

Encephalon

Description: A four-legged creature with an amorphous, shifting brain contained by cranial ribs and a quivering sheet of folding, retractable moist fascia. The brain accumulates or drains depending on how much the creature needs to think or rely upon raw strength. The puddles of grey brain slither around the environment retrieving information until they are reabsorbed.

Medium aberration, unaligned

Armour Class: 13 (natural armor)
Hit Points: 70 (12d8 + 12)
Speed: 30 ft.
Skills: Investigation +7, Perception +4
Senses: Darkvision 60 ft., passive Perception 14
Languages: understands Deep Speech but can't speak
Challenge: 2 (400XP)

Strength: +2 (up to +4)
Dexterity: +1
Constitution: +1
Intelligence: +4 (up to +6)
Wisdom: 0
Charisma: -1

Preemptive. When an Encephalon has +5 intelligence or more, it may take the dodge action as a reaction to an incoming attack. Dodge will remain active until the beginning of its next turn.

Amorphous Brain. A portion of the Encephalon's brain is amorphous and can drain, or re-enter, its body by using a bonus action. When its brain is contained in its body, it gains a +2 bonus to its Intelligence. When its brain is drained and slithering outside the body, the Encephalon gains a +2 bonus to its Strength.

Stolen Knowledge. If an Encephalon brain serpent successfully hits a target with a melee attack and then re-enters the Encephalon, the Encephalon has access to any information the snake gathered from its target(s) and may use these abilities at will, consuming the energy it would require to use them, such as spell slots or uses per rest, from the creature they have been stolen from.

Bite. *Melee Weapon Attack:* +4 (or +6) to hit, reach 5 ft. Hit: 13 (2d10 +2 (or +4)) piercing damage.

Brain Serpent

Description: Long coiled cords of spongy grey mousse that leak putrid-smelling oils in their wake.

Small aberration, unaligned

Armour Class: 10
Hit Points: 3
Speed: 20 ft.
Skills: --
Senses: Blindsight 120 ft.
Languages: --
Challenge: 1/8 (25XP)

Strength: -2
Dexterity: 0
Constitution: 0
Intelligence: +1
Wisdom: -1
Charisma: -2

Scouring Strike. *Melee Weapon Attack:* +2 to hit, reach 5 ft. Hit: 2 (1d4). The target must succeed on a DC 15 Wisdom saving throw or else the brain serpent learns everything it knows, including spells, class abilities and feats.

14. Mutation Row: Upper Level
This long, narrow 45 x 40 ft. room contains a 10 ft. wide 20 ft. high wrought iron skybridge that runs down the centre of the chamber towards a door. Between the walkway are six 15 x 15 x 20 ft. containment cells housing creatures for the Bloodbath Jubilee. Directly beneath the skybridge appears to be a lower walkway that mirrors the one above and runs between another

two doors. However, due to the position of the cells' caging, it is unclear how to access this lower path. There are control panels on the skybridge in front of each cell, containing two levers. The left lever opens up the caging on top of the cell, seemingly for feeding purposes, while the right lever opens up a portcullis within the cell along the wall, allowing the creatures to exit up a long ramp towards the temple's sandy Arena (1C). Five **ghouls**, adorned in vibrant tribal clothing, manage the facility and will attack any intruders. The ghouls are accompanied by a **cult fanatic** witch doctor named Xamen Bomasa. The moment Xamen or his ghouls become aware of the party, they will attack.

The left-hand side of the room contains a ventilated quartz tank housing thirty vampire pigeons, a bone terrarium containing a full-grown female Encephalon, and a bubbling, mud bath for an adolescent Bayouka.

The right-hand side of the room contains a cheesy-yellow spray all over the quartz walls and a fromagi inside: a dwarven runt infected by a cheddar-coloured fungal infection. The second cell contains a rearing venom pony, and the third cell contains a massive liger with a glass-encased cranium that shows its brain.

Xamen Bomasa

Description: A chocolate-skinned mad priest with bulging, accusatory eyes who runs the menagerie. Xamen is lean, muscular, has a pierced right nipple, and stands 6 ft. 1 in.

Xamen has the same stat block as a **cult fanatic** with a single exception. Instead of casting a spell or using his daggers, Xamen may instead choose to use Blood Voodoo (Recharge 5–6). So long as Xamen or his ghouls have drawn blood from a creature, he may perform a forbidden form of sympathetic magic, which involves Xamen harming himself in order to attempt to harm others. If his intended target fails a DC 15 Wisdom saving throw, the injury Xamen deals to himself also appears on the target creature's body. This may result in instant death depending on what injury Xamen inflicts on himself (e.g., slitting his own throat).

Swarm of Vampire Pigeons

Description: These doves have blood-red eyes and crimson speckles lining their wings. Though hard to see, their beaks are lined with tiny, razor-sharp fangs.

Medium swarm of Tiny beasts, unaligned

Armour Class: 13
Hit Points: 16 (6d4)
Speed: 40 ft., fly
Damage Resistances: bludgeoning, piercing, slashing
Condition Immunities: charmed, frightened, grappled, paralyzed, petrified, prone, restrained, stunned
Skills: Perception +1
Senses: passive Perception 11
Languages: --

Strength: -5
Dexterity: +4
Constitution: +3
Intelligence: -4
Wisdom: 0
Charisma: -2

Swarm. The swarm can occupy another creature's space and vice versa, and the swarm can move through any opening large enough for a pigeon. The swarm cannot regain hit points or gain temporary hit points.

Peck. Melee Weapon Attack: +5 to hit, reach 0 ft., one creature in the swarm's space. Hit: 8 (4d4) piercing damage, or 4 (2d4) piercing damage if the swarm has half of its hit points or fewer. Any creature who is hit by a pigeon's attack must make a DC 14 Constitution saving throw or else succumb to the curse of vampirism.

Bayouka

Description: The Bayouka resembles a fat, bony salamander with an engorged scorpion's tail. Its flesh is an intricate patchwork of hexagonal petals with bright green rivers of poison blood flowing in-between.

Medium monstrosity, unaligned

Armour Class: 15 (natural armor)
Hit Points: 85 (10d10 + 30)
Speed: 30 ft.
Damage Immunities: Poison
Condition Immunities: Poisoned
Senses: Darkvision 60 ft., passive Perception 11
Languages: -
Challenge: 4 (1,100 XP)

Strength: +2
Dexterity: +3
Constitution: +3
Intelligence: -4
Wisdom: +1
Charisma: -2

Regeneration. If the Bayouka is restrained or its tail is damaged by an attack, it can drop its tail and grow a new one in one round. Each new tail becomes increasingly deadly.

Viscid Tongue. As a bonus action, the Bayouka may use its tongue to try and ensnare a nearby creature. The Bayouka's adhesive tongue can reach up to 10 ft. When the tongue hits a target, it must make a DC 15 Strength saving throw. On a failed save, the target is pulled into the Bayouka's maw and is automatically hit by a free bite attack.

Poison Ooze. The Bayouka oozes a potent poison out of the gaps in its exoskeleton. Any creature that enters or starts its turn within 5 ft. of the Bayouka must make a DC 15 Constitution saving throw, taking 3 (1d6) poison damage on a failed save, or half as much on a successful one.

Multiattack. The Bayouka makes two attacks: one with its adhesive tongue and one with its tail.

Bite. Melee Weapon Attack: +5 to hit, reach 5 ft., one target. Hit: 7 (1d8 + 2) piercing damage and 3 (1d6) poison damage.

Tail. The Bayouka can attack with its tail as a melee weapon. *Melee Weapon Attack:* +5 to hit, reach 5 ft., one target. Hit: 7 (1d8 + 2) bludgeoning damage and must make a DC 15 Constitution saving throw, taking 14 (4d6) poison damage on a failed save, or half as much on a successful one. The tail's damage increases by 2d6 each time it regrows.

Fromagi

Description: This dwarven runt is beset by a highly infectious yellow fungus. At random intervals spurts and bursts of cheesy yellow liquid spray from the small dwarf's porous and inflamed flesh. The fluid deals acid damage and has a chance of spreading the virulent disease.

Small humanoid (dwarf), chaotic neutral

Armour Class: 12
Hit Points: 22 (5d6 + 5)
Speed: 25 ft.
Skills: Athletics +2, Survival +2
Condition Immunities: poisoned
Senses: Darkvision 60 ft., passive Perception 10
Languages: Common, Dwarvish
Challenge: 1/4 (50 XP)

Strength: 0
Dexterity: +1
Constitution: +1
Intelligence: -1
Wisdom: 0
Charisma: -2

Fungal Burst (Recharge 5–6). The Fromagi releases a burst of cheesy yellow liquid in a 10-foot cone. Each creature in that area must make a DC 11 Dexterity saving throw, taking 7 (2d6) acid damage on a failed save, or half as much damage on a successful one. Any creature that takes damage from this burst must make a DC 11 Constitution saving throw or become infected with the same fungal disease, causing their flesh to begin yellowing and runny sores to appear. Creatures already infected by the ailment take no damage from the spray.

Bite. Melee Weapon Attack: +2 to hit, reach 5 ft., one target. Hit: 4 (1d8) piercing damage.

Venom Pony

Description: This feathered pony has technicolour hooves doused in vivid green paralysing venom that bead to the tips of the sharp keratin.

Medium beast, unaligned

Armour Class: 12
Hit Points: 22 (4d8 + 4)
Speed: 50 ft.
Skills: Athletics +2
Senses: passive Perception 10
Languages: --
Challenge: 1/2 (100 XP)

Strength: +2
Dexterity: +3
Constitution: 1+1
Intelligence: -3
Wisdom: 0
Charisma: -3

Charge. If the venom pony moves at least 20 ft. straight toward a target and then hits it with a hooves attack on the same turn, the target takes an extra 6 (1d6 + 3) bludgeoning damage.

Hooves. Melee Weapon Attack: +5 to hit, reach 5 ft., one target. Hit: 6 (1d6 + 3) bludgeoning damage, plus the target must succeed on a DC 12 Constitution saving throw or become paralyzed for 1 minute. The target can repeat the saving throw at the end of each of its turns, ending the effect on a success.

Cranium Liger

Description: This stupefied liger has a septum piercing hooked up to electrical buzzing wires plugged into its glass-encased brain.

Large beast, unaligned

Armour Class: 12 (natural armor)
Hit Points: 52 (7d10 + 14)
Speed: 40 ft.
Skills: Perception +3, Stealth +6
Senses: Darkvision 60 ft., passive Perception 13
Languages: --
Challenge: 1 (200 XP)

Strength: +3
Dexterity: +2
Constitution: +2
Intelligence: -4
Wisdom: +1
Charisma: -2

Keen Smell. The tiger has advantage on Wisdom (Perception) checks that rely on smell.

Pounce. If the tiger moves at least 20 ft. straight toward a creature and then hits it with a claw attack on the same turn, that target must succeed on a DC 13 Strength saving throw or be knocked prone. If the target is prone, the tiger can make one bite attack against it as a bonus action.

Bite. Melee Weapon Attack: +5 to hit, reach 5 ft., one target. Hit: 8 (1d10 + 3) piercing damage.

Claw. Melee Weapon Attack: +5 to hit, reach 5 ft., one target. Hit: 7 (1d8 + 3) slashing damage. If the target is a creature, it must succeed on a DC 13 Strength saving throw or be knocked prone.

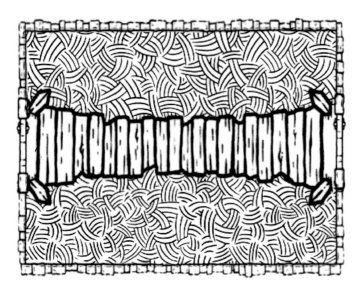

14.B Mutation Row: Lower Level
Beneath Mutation Row's (14) skybridge is a straight walkway that runs between two doors on either end. The door located beneath the upper room's entrance leads towards Underbridge (22) while the other is connected to the Sky Farmer's Grave (20). The only way this walkway can be accessed from above is by going through the damaged floor in the Mammothian Tomb (17).

15. The Devil's Hilt
Beyond the door at the far end of Mutation Row's (14) top floor is a 35 ft. perpendicular hallway that leads towards two doors, set equally spaced apart. Laying 10 ft. in either direction is a pressure plate. These plates are triggered by a weight of 25 lbs. or more, which causes darts to eject from holes concealed in the walls. Creatures hit by these darts must perform a DC 15 Constitution saving throw or else take 1d6 poison damage and suffer Fiend Susceptibility for one hour: disadvantage on all attacks against fiends, and fiends have advantage on all attacks against the affected target.

16. The Sunken Road
The door on the left side of the Devil's Hilt (15) exits into a bizarre room that smells of chlorine and ozone. The room contains a tiled slope, painted Zima blue, which descends towards metal grates. Unidentifiable numerals coat the sides of the deepening ramp. Three vagrant chrome-skinned **cambions** live here with a gagged prisoner: Gordon Saint. In a smashed-in crater of tiles, the cambions have placed burning logs and other dried detritus to burn for warmth. They will announce themselves to be "the Silverfish of Gosalamenten" and claim that any harm done to them is a crime against their great god. If they are approached, the cambions will attack any intruders, but if they think they are losing the battle (down to 25% health or less), they will break for the metal grates, which connect to a broken sewage system running beneath the dungeon from an age long past.

The prisoner, Gordon Saint, who has a deep Oklahoma drawl, is a scout. If he is freed, he will reveal that he mistakenly signed an infernal contract that gave Ovallo and his henchmen exclusive rights to his menagerie of travelling circus beasts. He is intent on saving his beloved creatures and escaping the god-forsaken facility. If Ovallo manages to interact with the creatures stored in Mutation Row (14), they will become docile and compliant for him, unless he orders them to attack on his behalf.

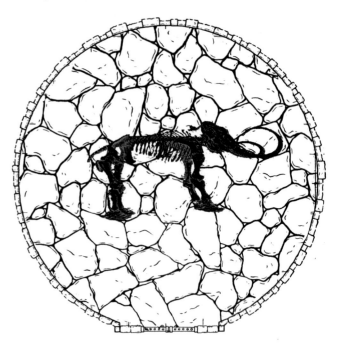

17. The Mammothian Tomb
The door on the right of the Devil's Hilt (15) leads towards an elephant graveyard. This circular room is 80 ft. in diameter and contains an enormous mammoth skeleton. This is where Phantrenei was left to decompose. Rotting leather is stretched between some of its exposed ribs and gummy, moldering underside. The eye cavities of the skull are 5 ft. in diameter. The smell inside the room is putrid and near unbearable.

If the room is explored, the heroes will discover three **hyenas**. These beasts are well-satiated by the rotting meat, and a DC 15 Wisdom (animal handling) check is enough to befriend the wary beasts. Otherwise, the hyenas will attack intruders.

Beyond one of the eye-sockets, the heroes may find a set of Moon Armour with a DC 12 Intelligence (investigation) check.

If creatures enter the corpse, they will find that the gut-laden leather is stretched and rotten, giving way to any weight greater than 150 pounds. The floor drops 30 ft. down into the Sky Farmer's Grave (20).

Moon Armour (Moonplate Set)
This heavy armour weighs 30 lbs. and requires a Strength score of 12 to don. Unlike other heavy armour, this armour does not give wearers' disadvantage on stealth, and provides an AC of 18. When in the presence of moonlight, by virtue of nature or otherwise, creatures donning the armour always have the spell *Blur* active.

18. Sewers
If the sewage system beneath the Sunken Road's (16) grates are explored, about 120 ft. down through the winding Byzantine

passages there is an expansive, lightless room, with a black void hanging where the ceiling should be. The floor is covered in 4 ft. of muddy groundwater and counts as difficult terrain. With a DC 10 Wisdom (perception) check, creatures may notice what looks like a free-floating gold ring hanging just above the cloudy water. In truth the gold ring is affixed to a transparent dragon-quartz hook hanging a mere foot above the water. If the ring is touched, creatures within 10 ft. of the hook must perform a DC 15 Dexterity saving throw or take 1d4 piercing damage, be embedded with hundreds of gossamer dragon barbs, and be swiftly reeled up 100 ft. to the Mound of the Fat God (19).

19. Mound of the Fat God

Gosalamanten, a **Nalfeshnee** who wears a Pierrot hill giant mask, sits in a sequestered cavern with a 15 ft. long titanium fishing rod. The room is misshapen and cavernous, but its rough dimensions are ~50 ft. in diameter. This massive, obese daemon sits feasting on a mound of faeces and ice-hardened vomit, muttering about its lack of seasoning to himself. Hidden in and amongst the cold sewage is a pair of Moon Boots, one of the three pieces of the Moonplate Set. The boots can be discovered with a DC 15 Intelligence (investigation) check.

Gosalamanten will be delighted at the prospect of live meals and will attempt to dismember and eat any he captures. Besides the fishing hole, there is only one exit to this chamber, in the form of a ventilation shaft on the ceiling that connects to the Gleam Gate Hold (6).

Forge

The ring attached to the fishing line is capable of flawlessly copying the writing or signature of any script the wearer has seen.

Moon Boots (Moonplate Set)

These boots allow the wearer to jump twice the distance they are typically capable of. In addition, the wearer takes half damage from falling.

20. The Sky Farmer's Grave

Upon entering this 40 x 40 x 40 ft. room and at the start of every round thereafter, have creatures perform a DC 12 Constitution saving throw. Creatures that fail their saving throw take 1d4 cold damage from the frigid temperatures inside. Within the

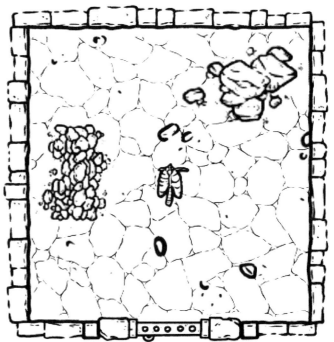

room there are thousands of small coals shedding faint light and an agrarian worker lying prostrated, frozen, and encased in ice. The farmer is clutching a *Levitation* spell scroll in his hand. Two large 500 lbs. mounds of rock, covered in char and impact craters, rest lying on the floor. The room does not appear to have a ceiling, but instead appears to be a starless night sky, and there is a barely audible wind flowing through the chamber. An invisible antigravitational layer of air sits in the room 10 ft. above the floor. Anything that enters this layer of air remains suspended and floating.

If the creatures manage to get the two fallen moons floating again and drag the sky farmer out of the room, completing the prophecy made by the parakeet-headed man on the Candlemoon Plains (10), they will discover a hatch beneath the skyfarmer's corpse, and a massive coffin will materialise adjacent to it. This coffin contains the Lunar Macuahuitl. The coffin seems to have indentations where armour and boots should be placed, but they are missing.

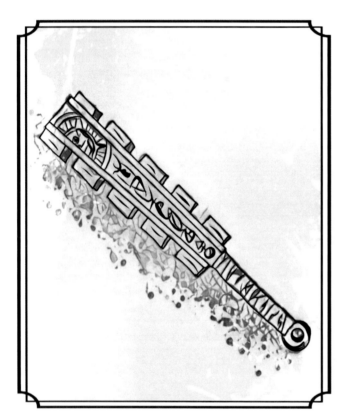

Lunar Macuahuitl (Moonplate Set)
This weapon deals 1d12 slashing damage and an additional 2d12 radiant damage whenever used in the presence of moonlight, regardless of its source.

21. The Festermile
Beneath the Sky Farmer's corpse there is a hidden hatch, below which is a ladder. The ladder lands upon a 600 ft. long stretch with a spire of treasure piled at its far end. The entire length is littered in skeletons and priceless artifacts. When creatures enter the room, hand all the players a folded piece of paper and tell them the following in no uncertain terms:

"Under no circumstances are you to disclose what any piece of paper given to you in this room says now, during or after the session."
Then, hand everyone an identical piece of paper that says:

"You are not infected."

While in the room, at the start of their turns, creatures must perform a DC 5 Wisdom (insight) check at the start of every round. If they fail their check, their character succumbs to paranoia, and perceives their fellow party members to be evil. In response, they must immediately attempt to flee or kill them due to psychotic illusion magics that plague their mind. To tell them this, hand any player that fails the check a new note. The note reads:

"Do everything in your character's power to kill your fellow party members or to escape them."

Note: The character's sanity will be restored exactly one hour later.

If the characters somehow manage to reach the hoard at the end of the room, they discover a human-leather bound chest. On its top is written the following phrase:

"Only open if you wish to know the truth"

Inside is a gold tablet that reads:

"The spell giants watch us through your skin, they have led you here to your death. They are inside you, reading this now. Resist their voices if you wish to live. Run!"

Players now fight to control their character as they gain consciousness of the player's patronage and existence: at the start of all character's subsequent turns, roll a Charisma check against a DC 10; if they succeed, they act of their own volition (DM's choice), otherwise direct their actions as normal. If players ever fail the check more than three turns in a row, their character becomes an autonomous NPC and control of them is forever broken: players must roll a new character.

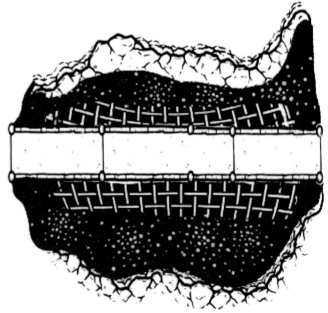

22. Underbridge
The lower level of Mutation Row (14B) contains a door, which opens upon a damp and undeveloped cave system. A slow wind passes through the cave which can be identified with a DC 13 Intelligence (nature) check. The breeze indicates the presence

of an access point beyond. The cave system is covered in an unidentifiable oily substance, which gives off an opalescent sheen under light. This substance is extremely flammable and used as a troll deterrent. It will form a deadly inferno if exposed to fire.

If the winding cave path is followed 120 ft., it eventually arrives at a 60 ft. causeway that connects two subterranean mountain ranges that are separated by a dizzying chasm. At the end of the causeway there are two sets of flanking staircases that descend towards the vertical, scaffolded city that hangs pitoned to the stone walls beneath the crossing: the famous troll city of Underbridge.

Sets of pressurised tubes connected to cubing butcher sieves allow the mutated trolls to migrate through the stone blisters and undulating rubber bladders that compose the narrow, vertical city. All told, two thousand trolls live in the folded layers of pumice and worm blubber that line the cave walls. The cave's surrounding greygrass hills and mounds are roaming billy goats that the trolls use for milk, cheese, and fermented meat products.

Beyond the causeway is a long, and wide-set freestanding staircase that ascends towards a jungle exit back three miles southwest of the Elephanzion. The staircase includes switchbacks and is 300 ft. of travel from the bottom to the top.

Room	Action	Points
1	• Discovering the viewing gallery runes • Succumbing to a Mammoth Squirrel head wound • Bypassing the Mammoth squirrels without initiating combat	+3 -1 +2
2	• Discovering the Buried Siege Tower • Identifying and avoiding the ladder trap • Triggering ladder trap • Defeating Sulphur Lamia	+2 +3 -2 +1
3	• Correctly identifying the rune pattern • Bypassing the exploding runes • Entering Death Lake	+1 +1 -3
4	• Escaping Death Lake alive	+3
5	• Not checking the hallways for traps • Falling into Chute Trap • Avoiding the Chute Trap	-1 -3 +3
6	• Solving the Gleam Gate Hold Chariot Puzzle on first attempt • Choosing the Candlemoon Plain Portal first	+3 +1
7	• Locating the Hidden Hatch • Entering Cicada Chute	+2 -1
8	• Solving the Tablet Riddle	+3
9	• Solving the Puzzle Cube Riddle • Discovering the exit to the Crystal Gaol • Drinking the Troll Tequila • Eating the Tequila Worm	+3 +2 +1 +1
10	• Exiting the Candlemoon Plains in 16 hours or less	+2
11	• Preemptively using Detect Good & Evil or Identify on the magic item	+3
12	• Save Patrick	+1
13	• Save Raithvus	+2
14	• Defeat Xamen & his Ghouls	+2
15	• Avoid Trap • Hit by Trap	+2 -2
16	• Avoid combat with Cambions • Rescue Gordon Saint	+2 +2
17	• Find Moon Armour • Discover the drop to the Skyfarmer's Grave	+3 +2
18	• Avoid Dragon Barb Trap	+3
19	• Find Moon Boots	+3
20	• Solve Skyfarmer Puzzle • Find Lunar Macuahuitl	+3 +3
21	• Reach the Human-Leather Chest	+4
22	• Exit the Elephanzion past Underbridge • Kill 3+ Trolls	+3 +3

Additional Points:

Rescue Gordon Saint	+50
Retrieve all Three Pieces of the Moonplate Set	+50
Rescue Raithvus Spane	+50
Bring Back 6 Troll Ears	+50
Kill Ovallo	+50

4 Characters Escape Alive	+100
3 Characters Escape Alive	+80
2 Characters Escape Alive	+60
1 Character Escapes Alive	+40

Characters lost within the first 20 minutes	-20
Characters lost within the second 20 minutes	-15
Characters lost within the third 20 minutes	-10
Characters lost within the fourth 20 minutes	-5
Characters lost within the fifth 20 minutes	-3

In order to avoid negative scoring, 100 points should be added to each team's total.

Elephanzion Tournament Rules

The following scoring guidelines are straightforward and should allow the governing referee to check off actions that score points or penalties accordingly. Points can be tallied once the module concludes.

This tournament is designed to be played by a team of four, 3rd-level characters of the following races and classes:

- human, battle master fighter
- hill dwarf, life cleric
- halfling, assassin rogue
- high elf, divination wizard.

No variant rules are allowed and only the Player's Handbook may be used during character creation. The players have exactly 120 minutes to complete the dungeon to the best of their ability.

OPEN GAME LICENSE Version 1.0a

The following text is the property of Wizards of the Coast, Inc. and is Copyright 2000 Wizards of the Coast, Inc ("Wizards"). All Rights Reserved.

1. De nitions: (a)"Contributors" means the copyright and/ or trademark owners who have contributed Open Game Content; (b)"Derivative Material" means copyrighted material including derivative works and translations (including into other computer languages), potation, modi cation, correction, addition, extension, upgrade, improvement, compilation, abridgment or other form in which an existing work may be recast, transformed or adapted; (c) "Distribute" means to reproduce, license, rent, lease, sell, broadcast, publicly display, transmit or otherwise distribute; (d)"Open Game Content" means the game mechanic and includes the methods, procedures, processes and routines to the extent such content does not embody the Product Identity and is an enhancement over the prior art and any additional content clearly identi ed as Open Game Content by the Contributor, and means any work covered by this License, including translations and derivative works under copyright law, but speci cally excludes Product Identity. (e) "Product Identity" means product and product line names, logos and identifying marks including trade dress; artifacts; creatures characters; stories, storylines, plots, thematic elements, dialogue, incidents, language, artwork, symbols, designs, depictions, likenesses, formats, poses, concepts, themes and graphic, photographic and other visual or audio representations; names and descriptions of characters, spells, enchantments, personalities, teams, personas, likenesses and special abilities; places, locations, environments, creatures, equipment, magical or supernatural abilities or effects, logos, symbols, or graphic designs; and any other trademark or registered trademark clearly identi ed as Product identity by the owner of the Product Identity, and which speci cally excludes the Open Game Content; (f) "Trademark" means the logos, names, mark, sign, motto, designs that are used by a Contributor to identify itself or its products or the associated products contributed to the Open Game License by the Contributor (g) "Use", "Used" or "Using" means to use, Distribute, copy, edit, format, modify, translate and otherwise create Derivative Material of Open Game Content. (h) "You" or "Your" means the licensee in terms of this agreement.

2. The License: This License applies to any Open Game Content that contains a notice indicating that the Open Game Content may only be Used under and in terms of this License. You must af x such a notice to any Open Game Content that you Use. No terms may be added to or subtracted from this License except as described by the License itself. No other terms or conditions may be applied to any Open Game Content distributed using this License.

3. Offer and Acceptance: By Using the Open Game Content You indicate Your acceptance of the terms of this License.

4. Grant and Consideration: In consideration for agreeing to use this License, the Contributors grant You a perpetual, worldwide, royalty\free, non-exclusive license with the exact terms of this License to Use, the Open Game Content.

5. Representation of Authority to Contribute: If You are contributing original material as Open Game Content, You represent that Your Contributions are Your original creation and/or You have suf cient rights to grant the rights conveyed by this License.

6. Notice of License Copyright: You must update the COPYRIGHT NOTICE portion of this License to include the exact text of the COPYRIGHT NOTICE of any Open Game Content You are copying, modifying or distributing, and You must add the title, the copyright date, and the copyright holder's name to the COPYRIGHT NOTICE of any original Open Game Content you Distribute.

7. Use of Product Identity: You agree not to Use any Product Identity, including as an indication as to compatibility, except as expressly licensed in another, independent Agreement with the owner of each element of that Product Identity. You agree not to indicate compatibility or co\adaptability with any Trademark or Registered Trademark in conjunction with a work containing Open Game Content except as expressly licensed in another, independent Agreement with the owner of such Trademark or Registered Trademark. The use of any Product Identity in Open Game Content does not constitute a challenge to the ownership of that Product Identity. The owner of any Product Identity used in Open Game Content shall retain all rights, title and interest in and to that Product Identity.

8. Identification: If you distribute Open Game Content You must clearly indicate which portions of the work that you are distributing are Open Game Content.

9. Updating the License: Wizards or its designated Agents may publish updated versions of this License. You may use any authorized version of this License to copy, modify and distribute any Open Game Content originally distributed under any version of this License.

10. Copy of this License: You MUST include a copy of this License with every copy of the Open Game Content You Distribute.

11. Use of Contributor Credits: You may not market or advertise the Open Game Content using the name of any Contributor unless You have written permission from the Contributor to do so.

12. Inability to Comply: If it is impossible for You to comply with any of the terms of this License with respect to some or all of the Open Game Content due to statute, judicial order, or governmental regulation then You may not Use any Open Game Material so affected.

13. Termination: This License will terminate automatically if You fail to comply with all terms herein and fail to cure such breach within 30 days of becoming aware of the breach. All sublicenses shall survive the termination of this License.

14. Reformation: If any provision of this License is held to be unenforceable, such provision shall be reformed only to the extent necessary to make it enforceable.

15. COPYRIGHT NOTICE

Open Game License v 1.0a Copyright 2000, Wizards of the Coast, LLC. System Reference Document 5.1 Copyright 2016, Wizards of the Coast, Inc.; Authors Mike Mearls, Jeremy Crawford, Chris Perkins, Rodney Thompson, Peter Lee, James Wyatt, Robert J. Schwalb, Bruce R. Cordell, Chris Sims, and Steve Townshend, based on original material by E. Gary Gygax and Dave Arneson.

The Elephanzion, Copyright 2023, The Bugbear Brothers

END OF LICENSE

Made in United States
North Haven, CT
26 December 2024

63526837R00015